لومڑی اور سارس

ایک ایسپ کی روایتی حکایت

The Fox and the Crane

- an Aesop's Fable

retold by Dawn Casey

illustrated by Jago

Urdu translation by Qamar Zamani

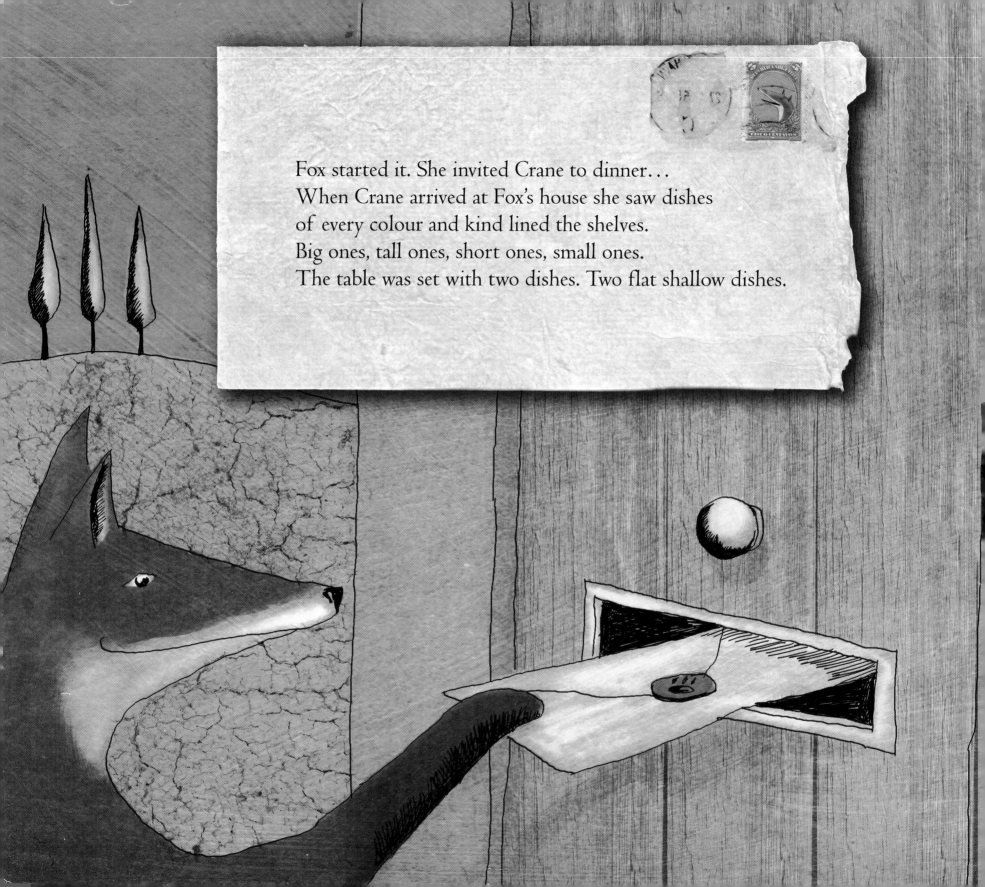

Fox started it. She invited Crane to dinner...
When Crane arrived at Fox's house she saw dishes
of every colour and kind lined the shelves.
Big ones, tall ones, short ones, small ones.
The table was set with two dishes. Two flat shallow dishes.

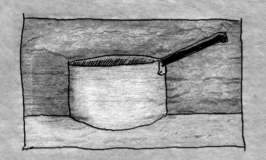

لومڑی نے ہی شروعات کی۔ اُس نے سارس کو کھانے کی دعوت دی۔۔۔

جب سارس لومڑی کے گھر پہنچا تو اُس نے دیکھا کہ الماری کے تختوں پر ہر رنگ اور قسم کی رکابیاں سجی ہوئی ہیں۔ کچھ بڑی، کچھ لمبی، کچھ چھوٹی اور کچھ ننھی سی۔

میز پر دور کابیاں رکھی تھیں۔ دو چپٹی اور اُتھلی رکابیاں۔

سارس نے اپنی لمبی پتلی چونچ سے اُن پر بہت مُنہ مارا اور بہت کوشش کی لیکن اِس تمام کوشش کے باوجود وہ اُس شوربے کا ایک گھونٹ بھی نہ پی سکا۔

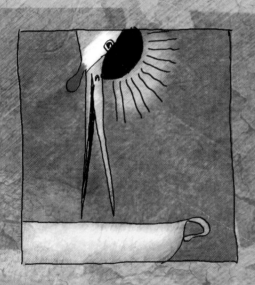  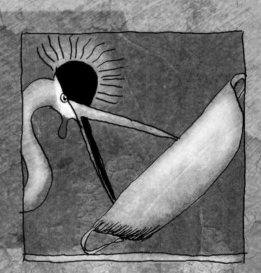

Crane pecked and she picked with her long thin beak. But no matter how hard she tried she could not get even a sip of the soup.

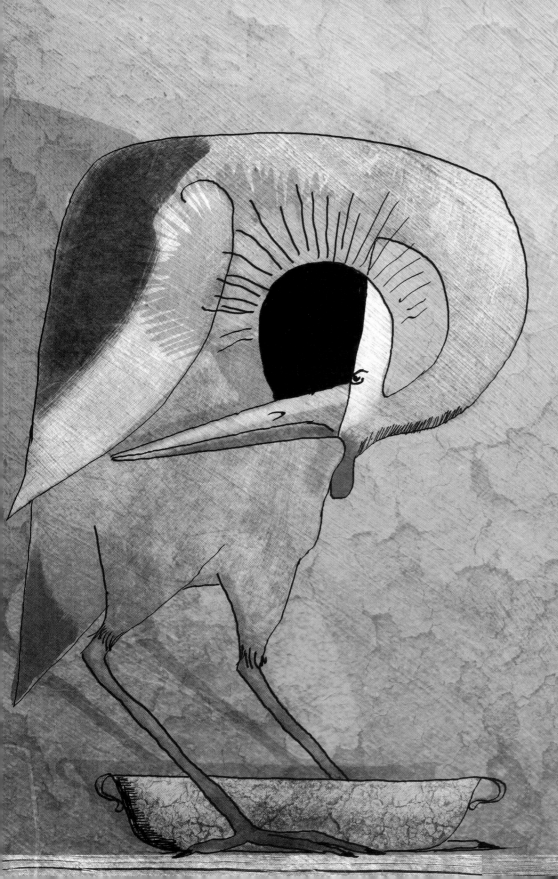

لومڑی نے سارس کو مشکل میں پھنسے ہوا دیکھا اور
چپکے چپکے ہنسی۔ اُس نے اپنا شوربہ اُٹھا کر ہونٹوں سے لگا لیا
اور سڑاپ، سڑاپ کر کے سارا شوربہ پی گئی۔
"واہ واہ، بہت مزیدار!" اُس نے ندیدے پن سے کہا
اور اپنا پنجہ اُٹھا کر اپنی مونچھیں پونچھنے لگی۔
"اور، سارس، تم نے تو اپنا شوربہ چکھا بھی نہیں۔"
لومڑی نے بناوٹ سے مُسکرا کر کہا
"مجھے واقعی افسوس ہے کہ یہ تمہیں پسند نہیں آیا۔"
اُس نے پوری کوشش سے اپنی ہنسی دباتے ہوئے کہا۔

Fox watched Crane struggling and sniggered.
She lifted her own soup to her lips, and
with a SIP, SLOP, SLURP she lapped it all
up. "Ahhhh, delicious!" she scoffed, wiping
her whiskers with the back of her paw.
"Oh Crane, you haven't touched your soup,"
said Fox with a smirk. "I AM sorry you
didn't like it," she added, trying not to snort
with laughter.

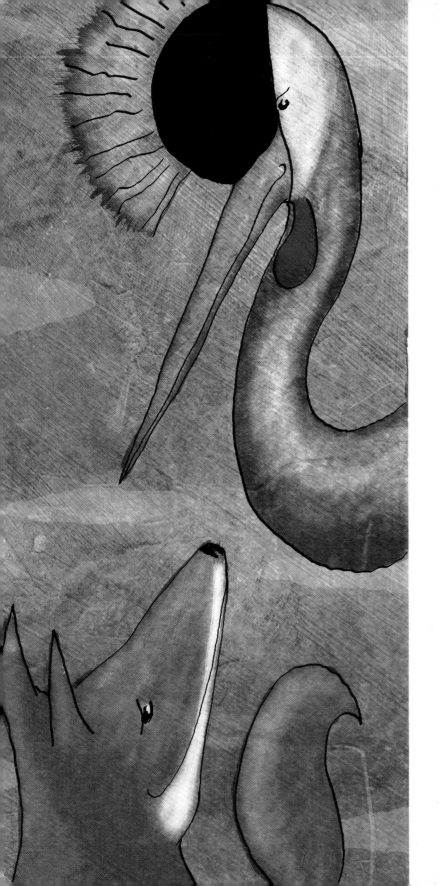

سارس کچھ نہیں بولا۔ اُس نے کھانے کی طرف دیکھا۔
پھر اُس نے رکابی پر نظر ڈالی۔ اُس نے لومڑی کی طرف دیکھااور مسکرایا۔
”عزیزلومڑی، تمہاری مہربانی کا بہت بہت شکریہ“
سارس نے بے حد نرمی سے کہا ”مہربانی کرکے مجھے بھی کچھ کرنے کا موقع دو۔
تُم میرے گھر کھانے کے لئے آؤ۔“

جب لومڑی اُس کے گھر پہنچی تو کھڑکی کھلی ہوئی تھی۔
ایک اشتہاانگیز خوشبو ہوا کے ساتھ باہر آرہی تھی۔
لومڑی نے اپنی تھوتھنی اُوپر کی اور سونگھنے لگی۔
اُس کے مُنہ میں پانی بھر آیا۔ اُس کے پیٹ میں گڑگڑاہٹ ہونے لگی۔
اُس نے اپنے ہونٹ چاٹ لئے۔

Crane said nothing. She looked at the meal. She looked at the dish. She looked at Fox, and smiled.
"Dear Fox, thank you for your kindness," said Crane politely. "Please let me repay you – come to dinner at my house."

When Fox arrived the window was open. A delicious smell drifted out. Fox lifted her snout and sniffed. Her mouth watered. Her stomach rumbled. She licked her lips.

”میری عزیز لومڑی۔ اندر آجاؤ“
سارس نے اپنے پر خوبصورتی سے پھیلاتے ہوئے کہا۔
لومڑی سارس سے آگے بڑھ گئی۔ اُس نے دیکھا کہ ہر رنگ
اور قسم کی رکابیاں اور برتن الماری کے تختوں پر سجے ہوئے ہیں۔
سرخ رنگ کے، نیلے رنگ کے، پرانے اور نئے۔
میز پر دو برتن لگے ہوئے تھے۔
دو لمبے اور پتلے برتن۔

"My dear Fox, do come in," said Crane,
extending her wing graciously.
Fox pushed past. She saw dishes of
every colour and kind lined the shelves.
Red ones, blue ones, old ones, new ones.
The table was set with two dishes.
Two tall narrow dishes.

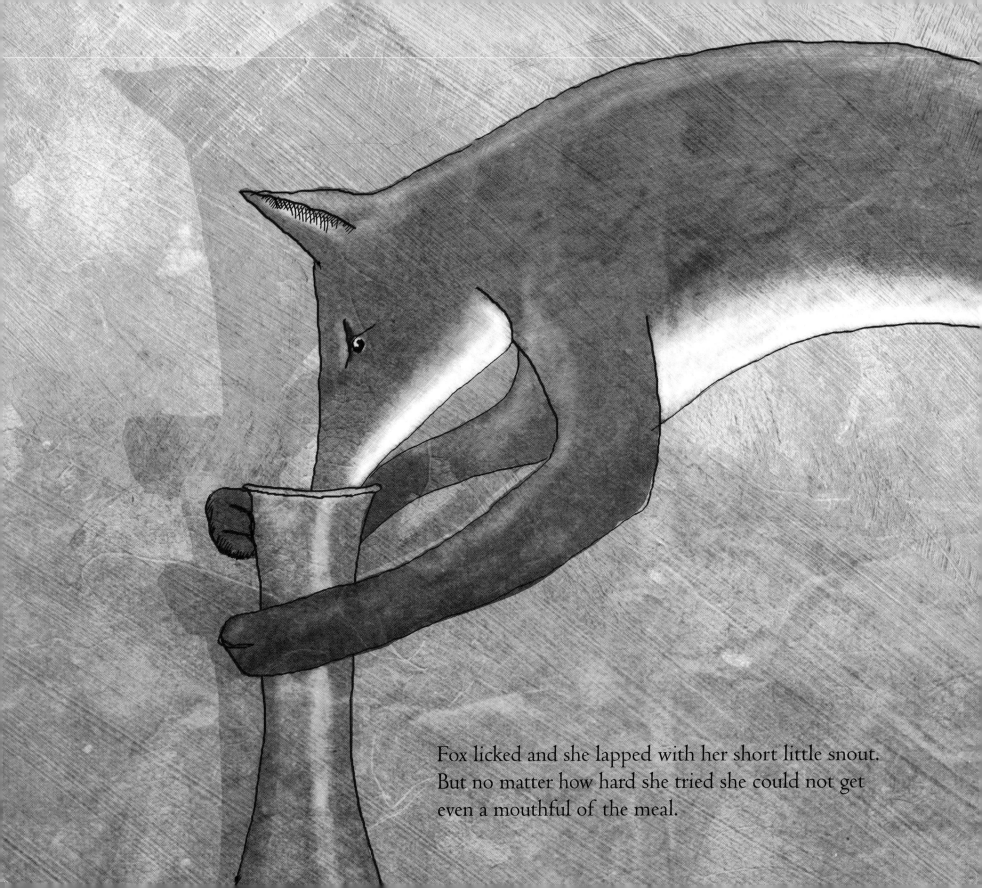

Fox licked and she lapped with her short little snout.
But no matter how hard she tried she could not get
even a mouthful of the meal.

لومڑی نے اپنی چھوٹی سی تھوتھنی سے چاٹنے کی اور پینے کی کوشش کی۔
لیکن اُس کی انتہائی کوشش کے باوجود وہ کھانے کا ایک نوالہ بھی نہیں لے سکی۔

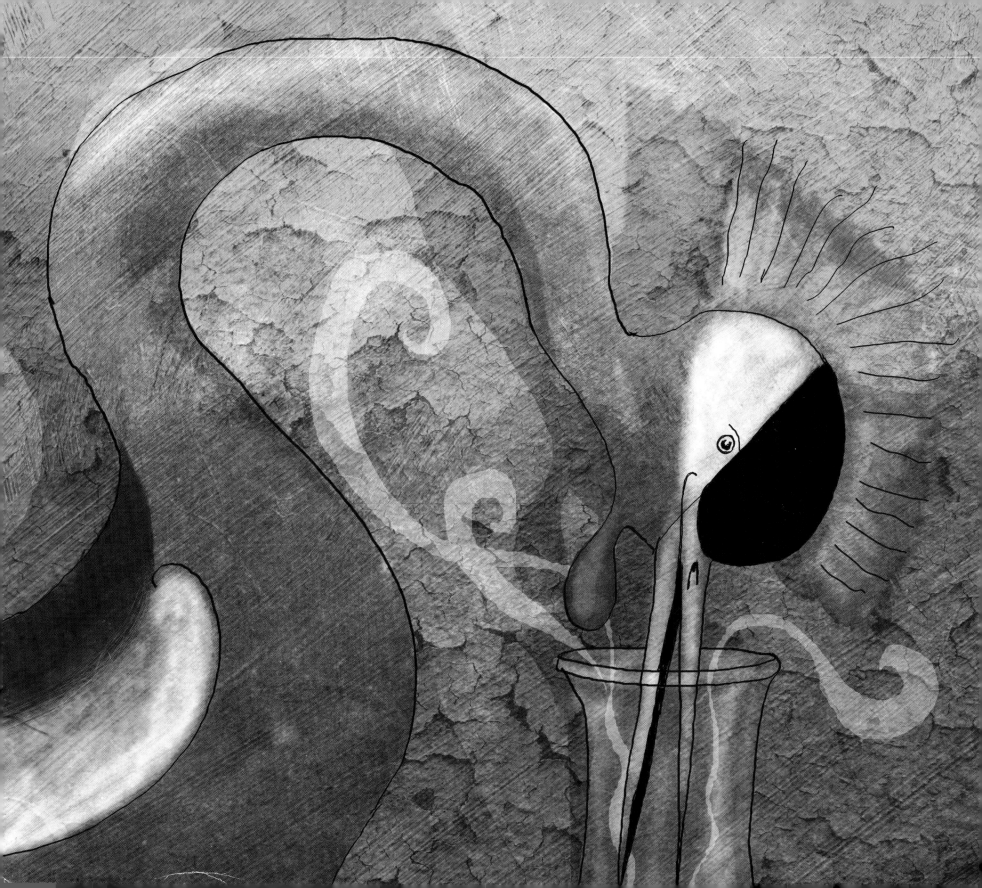

سارس نے اپنا کھانا اطمینان سے، ہر نوالے کا مزہ لے لے کر کھایا۔

"عزیز لومڑی، تمہارے آنے کا بہت بہت شکریہ" وہ مسکرایا۔

"تمہاری مہربانی کا بدلہ دے کر مجھے بے حد خوشی ہوئی۔"

لومڑی کا پیٹ بھوک کے مارے گڑ گڑا رہا تھا۔

اور جب وہ گھر پہنچی تو اُس وقت بھی بھوکی تھی۔

Crane ate her meal very slowly, savouring every mouthful.
"Dear Fox, thank you so much for coming," she smiled,
"it has been a pleasure to repay your kindness."

Fox's tummy gurgled and grumbled.
And when she went home, she was still hungry.

The Fox and the Crane

Writing Activity:
Read the story. Explain that we can write our own fable by changing the characters.

Discuss the different animals you could use, bearing in mind what different kinds of dishes they would need! For example, instead of the fox and the crane you could have a tiny mouse and a tall giraffe.

Write an example together as a class, then give the children the opportunity to write their own. Children who need support could be provided with a writing frame.

Art Activity:
Dishes of every colour and kind! Create them from clay, salt dough, play dough… Make them, paint them, decorate them…

Maths Activity:
Provide a variety of vessels: bowls, jugs, vases, mugs… Children can use these to investigate capacity:

Compare the containers and order them from smallest to largest.

Estimate the capacity of each container.

Young children can use non-standard measures e.g. 'about 3 beakers full'.

Check estimates by filling the container with coloured liquid ('soup') or dry lentils.

Older children can use standard measures such as a litre jug, and measure using litres and millilitres. How near were the estimates?

Label each vessel with its capacity.

The Ruler of the Forest

Writing Activity:
Children can write their own fables by changing the setting of this story. Think about what kinds of animals you would find in a different setting. For example how about 'The Ruler of the Arctic' starring an arctic fox and a polar bear!

Storytelling Activity:
Draw a long path down a roll of paper showing the route Fox took through the forest. The children can add their own details, drawing in the various scenes and re-telling the story orally with model animals.

If you are feeling ambitious you could chalk the path onto the playground so that children can act out the story using appropriate noises and movements! (They could even make masks to wear, decorated with feathers, woollen fur, sequin scales etc.)

Music Activity:
Children choose a forest animal. Then select an instrument that will make a sound that matches the way their animal looks and moves. Encourage children to think about musical features such as volume, pitch and rhythm. For example a loud, low, plodding rhythm played on a drum could represent an elephant.

Children perform their animal sounds. Can the class guess the animal?

Children can play their pieces in groups, to create a forest soundscape.

جنگل کا بادشاہ

ایک چینی روایتی حکایت

The Ruler of the Forest
– a Chinese Fable

retold by Dawn Casey

illustrated by Jago

Urdu translation by Qamar Zamani

لومڑی جنگل میں چلی جا رہی تھی جب اُس نے لمبی گھاس میں کسی کے حرکت کرنے کی آواز سُنی۔

رَسل   کوئی بڑی چیز۔

بلنک   کوئی پیلی آنکھوں والی چیز۔

فلیش   کوئی چاقو کی طرح دانتوں والی چیز۔

Fox was walking in the forest when she heard something moving in the long grass.
RUSTLE   Something big.
BLINK   Something with yellow eyes.
FLASH   Something with teeth like knives.

"صبح بخیر، ننھی لومڑی" شیر نے ہنس کر کہااور اُس کے مُنہ میں علاوہ دانتوں کے اور کچھ نہیں تھا۔

لومڑی نے تھوک نگلا۔

"تم سے مل کر بہت خوشی ہوئی۔" شیر نے ہلکی غراہٹ سے کہا۔

"مجھے بس ابھی بھوک لگنا شروع ہوئی تھی۔"

لومڑی نے تیزی سے سوچا "تمہاری ہمت کیسے ہوئی!" وہ بولی۔

"کیا تمہیں نہیں معلوم کہ اس جنگل میں میری حیثیت بادشاہ کی ہے؟"

"تم؟ جنگل کی بادشاہ؟" شیر بولااور اُس نے زبردست قہقہہ لگایا۔

"اگر تمہیں یقین نہیں آتا۔" لومڑی نے بڑی شان سے کہا "میرے پیچھے چل کر دیکھو

اور تمہیں پتہ چل جائے گا۔ سب مجھ سے ڈرتے ہیں۔"

"یہ تو مجھے ضرور دیکھنا ہے۔" شیر بولا۔

لہذا لومڑی نے جنگل میں چہل قدمی شروع کر دی۔ شیر بڑے غرور کے ساتھ اُس کے پیچھے چل رہا تھا۔ دُم اُٹھی ہوئی تھی۔ جب تک۔۔۔۔

"Good morning little fox," Tiger grinned, and his mouth was nothing but teeth.
Fox gulped.
"I am pleased to meet you," Tiger purred. "I was just beginning to feel hungry."
Fox thought fast. "How dare you!" she said. "Don't you know I'm the Ruler of the Forest?"
"You! Ruler of the Forest?" said Tiger, and he roared with laughter.
"If you don't believe me," replied Fox with dignity, "walk behind me and you'll see –
everyone is scared of me."
"This I've got to see," said Tiger.
So Fox strolled through the forest. Tiger followed behind proudly, with his tail held high, until…

اِس کو اک!

ایک بہت بڑا اکنڈا نما چونچ والا عقاب! لیکن عقاب نے ایک نظر شیر پر ڈالی اور

اُڑ تا ہوا درختوں میں چھپ گیا۔

”دیکھا؟“ لومڑی نے کہا ”ہر ایک مجھ سے ڈرتا ہے!“

”یقین نہیں آتا!“ شیر بولا۔

لومڑی جنگل میں آگے بڑھتی گئی۔ شیر بھی آہستہ قدموں سے اُس کے پیچھے چلا۔

اُس کی دُم ذرا نیچے جھک گئی تھی۔ جب تک...

SQUAWK!
A huge hook-beaked hawk! But the hawk took
one look at Tiger and flapped into the trees.
"See?" said Fox. "Everyone is scared of me!"
"Unbelievable!" said Tiger.
            Fox strode on through the forest.
            Tiger followed behind lightly,
            with his tail drooping slightly,
            until...

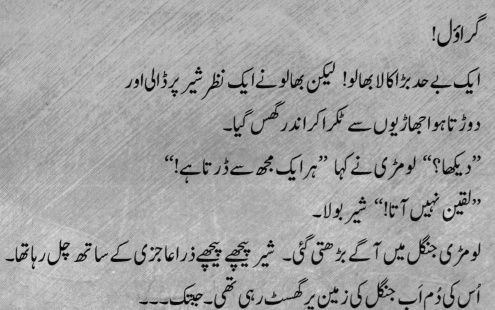

گر اوّل!

ایک بے حد بڑا کالا بھالو! لیکن بھالو نے ایک نظر شیر پر ڈالی اور دوڑتا ہوا جھاڑیوں سے ٹکرا کر اندر گھس گیا۔

"دیکھا؟" لومڑی نے کہا "ہر ایک مجھ سے ڈرتا ہے!"

"یقین نہیں آتا!" شیر بولا۔

لومڑی جنگل میں آگے بڑھتی گئی۔ شیر پیچھے پیچھے ذرا عاجزی کے ساتھ چل رہا تھا۔ اُس کی دُم اَب جنگل کی زمین پر گھسٹ رہی تھی۔ جبتک۔۔۔۔

GROWL!
A big black bear! But the bear took one look
at Tiger and crashed into the bushes.
"See?" said Fox. "Everyone is scared of me!"
"Incredible!" said Tiger.
Fox marched on through the forest. Tiger
followed behind meekly, with his tail
dragging on the forest floor, until…

ہـس س س!

ایک لہراتا ہوا چکنا سانپ! لیکن سانپ نے ایک نظر شیر پر ڈالی اور رینگتا ہوا گھنی جھاڑیوں میں غائب ہو گیا۔

"دیکھا؟" لومڑی نے کہا۔ "ہر ایک مجھ سے ڈرتا ہے!"

HISSSSSSS!
A slinky slidey snake! But the snake took one look at Tiger and slithered into the undergrowth. "SEE?" said Fox. "EVERYONE IS SCARED OF ME!"

"I do see," said Tiger, "you are the Ruler of the Forest and I am your humble servant."
"Good," said Fox. "Then, be gone!"

And Tiger went, with his tail between his legs.

"میں نے دیکھ لیا ہے" شیر بولا "آپ ہی اِس جنگل کی حکمران ہیں اور میں آپ کا ادنیٰ خادم ہوں۔"

"ٹھیک ہے" لومڑی نے کہا "اَب چلتے بنو!"

اور شیر اپنی دُم دونوں ٹانگوں کے بیچ میں چھپا کر چلا گیا۔

"جنگل کی حکمران۔" لومڑی نے مسکراکر کہا۔ اور اُس کی مسکراہٹ ایک ہنسی میں تبدیل ہو گئی
اور پھر یہ ہنسی قہقہے میں بدل گئی۔ اور وہ اپنے گھر تک زور زور سے قہقہے لگاتی گئی۔

"Ruler of the Forest," said Fox to herself with a smile. Her smile grew into a grin, and her grin grew into a giggle, and Fox laughed out loud all the way home.

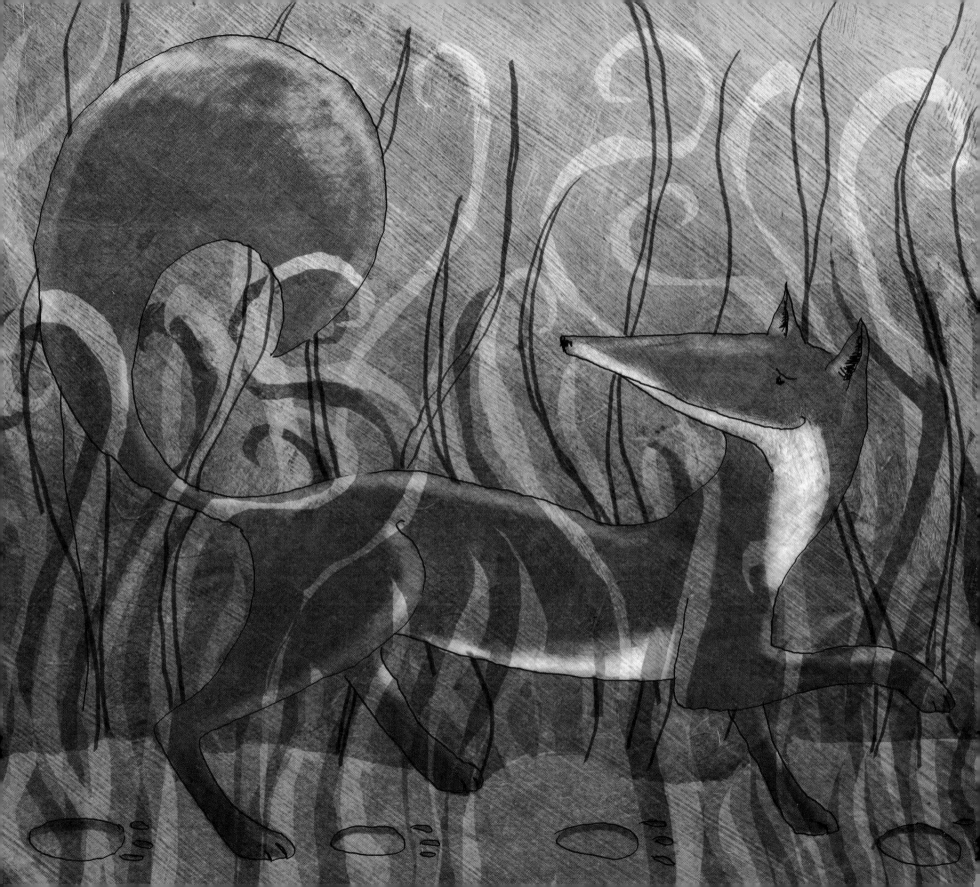

To my Nana, with love - DC
For my wife, Alex - J

First published in 2006 by Mantra Lingua Ltd
Global House, 303 Ballards Lane
London N12 8NP
www.mantralingua.com

A CIP record for this book is available from the British Library